# Together Forever

Eileen DiStasio-Clark

*With Great Love and Appreciation to those who Have and Do Bless My Life*


### *My Family:*

*Joseph DeStasio Sr. & Miriam Lucille Baragone DeStasio, My Late Parents.*

*Andrea Jean DeStasio McIntosh, My Older Sister and their Family.*

*Joseph DeStasio Jr., My Younger and Only Brother and their Family.*

*Donna Marie DeStasio Wagner, My Younger Sister and their Family.*


### *My Children:*

*Eileen, Rebekah, Rachel, S. Michael,*

*Jennifer, Sharon, Tara, Stephanie,*

*Apryll, Mikaelah, & M. Trevor*

*and THEIR Families!!*

# Acknowledgments

First and foremost, I express, deeply, my sincere gratitude to our Heavenly Father for blessing me with the gift and talent of writing! I know I could not do what I do without His assistance.

I also want to acknowledge and express gratitude to the members of my birth family—Joseph Sr., Miriam, Andrea, Joseph Junior, and Donna. All the experiences of my childhood years, experiences that taught me so very much and enabled me to reveal my true self to myself, came about through my experiences and relationships with them.

And, of course, it goes without saying, but I will say it anyway: I also want to acknowledge and note my gratitude to my children, Eileen, Rebekah, Rachel, S. Michael, Jennifer, Sharon, Tara, Stephanie, Apryll, Mikaelah, and M. Trevor, and their families! Through multiple things they said to me, over multiple years, I finally came to the realization that Heavenly Father gave me the gift of writing and opened the doors to these experiences because He knew that by sharing them with others, others could feel His love too.

And He definitely wants us all to know that He, Heavenly Father, Heavenly Mother, and Jehovah truly do loves us!!!

# Introduction

There are sixteen books in this series, which I refer to as *"The Ellie Series."* All of the characters in these stories portray real people from my life. The main characters depict the members of my family: Daddy is my daddy; Mommy is my mommy; Jeannie is my older sister; Junior is my brother; Maria is my younger sister; and Ellie is me. Now, those are not our actual first names, but they do reference us.

The first story in the series presents our Heavenly Father's Plan of Salvation and takes place in the Pre-Earth World. Now, of course, because we all—when we were born—received what is known as The Veil of Forgetfulness, I do not actually remember everything from or about the Pre-Earth World, but I do know about and understand it from much study and worship as a member of The Church of Jesus Christ of Latter-Day Saints, and memories restored to me through the Holy Spirit. So, from this story there is much truth to be learned.

The last story in the series is set in the Post-Mortal World, and presents a depiction of what happens to us after this life. Again, because I have not gone there yet, I cannot say I 'remember' this. But, I have also learned about the Post-Mortal World from much study and worship as a member of The Church of Jesus Christ of Latter-Day Saints.

All of the other stories are based on true events from my life; events that actually occurred when and how they are depicted in these stories. I chose these events because they are among the many occurrences in my life that presented, or revealed that which I already knew without having to be taught, Principles of Eternal Truths.

Also, I chose these events as the settings for my stories because they depict wonderful learning moments from my childhood and adolescent years, lessons that have blessed and benefited me throughout the whole of my life and will forever continue to do so. Also, through these great truths and their consequences in my life, I have been able to share them with many others, whose lives have also been blessed by them.

So, please read and enjoy, then care and share the messages and stories with others!!

Now, there are also a couple of things you can look for:

In each story, the title of the previous story is presented in *italicized* form, the title of the next story is presented in *Capitalized Italicized* form, and the title of the story being read is presented in **emboldened** form.

Also, every story has at least one word that is uncommon or 'created.'

So, as you read, search, find, and have fun!

# Together Forever

As Ellie hiked up Y Mountain Trail, she realized, with a bit of sadness and a bundle of joy, that that was probably—though she hoped only possibly—the last time she would ever have the opportunity to walk to Y Mountain. She had done so—hiked up the trail— many times in the three years that she had been at Brigham Young University, aka BYU. Now, of course, while the trail was said to be just 1.1 miles, for Ellie, it had always been at least two or more miles, and yes, that was just going up! It was even longer coming down. You see, Ellie was not just a hiker; she was an explorer! So, anytime something caught her attention, no matter what it was or where it was, on or off the trail, she had to go and investigate it.

Sometimes those investigations uncovered treasures. Well, at least that was what Ellie called them. Sometimes those investigations uncovered threats. Well, at least that was what Ellie called those. Sometimes those investigations uncovered nothing, well, at least that was what Ellie thought. But they always provided intrigue and enjoyment for Ellie, and that was why she loved to investigate while she hiked.

So, as you should be able to see by now, she really did, and does, love hiking! And the Y Mountain Trail was one of her most favorite trails to hike. Of course...

'Wait! Wait! Wait!' You are screaming at me. 'You cannot just say she uncovered treasures, threats, or nothing and then go on without explaining what those treasures, threats, and nothing were. That would be not nice!'

Oh! Well, okay. Then, I guess we should go take one of those hikes with her so you can see what I mean. Do you want to do that? You do?! Okay, then let us be going back... uh... let us go back to her first summer in Provo. Provo, Utah, that is, when she took her very first hike up Y Mountain Trail. Are you ready? You are?! Okay, then let us be hiking.

"Oh, wowzerx-trouzers!" Ellie exclaimed as she and Lucy, one of her roommates, made their way up Y Mountain Trail! "This is unbelievably awesome!!"

"I am glad you like it," was Lucy's response, "but I am not surprised that you do. I do not know anyone who loves to walk, everywhere, as much as you do."

With a broad smile, indicating that she greatly appreciated Lucy's acknowledgement of her love for walking everywhere. Ellie said, "Yeah, you got that right! And I especially love hiking up steep hills."

"Well," Lucy said, "I do not know about you, but I would not call this a hill. Steep? Yes! Just a hill? NO!! This is a true mountain!"

As they laughed at Lucy's emotionally adorned comment, they continued their way up the trail. When they were just about halfway between the bottom and the top of the mountain, all of a sudden, Ellie said, with an expression of curious awe, "Oh my goodness! What is that?"

"What is what?" Lucy asked.

"That," Ellie replied, pointing to something that was sticking up out of the ground. So curious was she that she left the trail and walked over to it. Once there, she stooped down and picked it up. Well, she tried to pick it up, but whatever it was, it was stuck in the dirt.

"What is it?" Lucy asked as she walked up behind Ellie.

"I do not know," Ellie uttered, as she began brushing the dirt away from it. "I can only see the top of it because it is stuck in the dirt. I want to say it looks like a rock, but I have never seen a rock that looks like this. It looks like it is speckled with orange crystals."

As Lucy looked closer, she said, "Well, I have never seen a rock like that either, but I don't know what else it could be." Then as she searched around the trees for a thick stick, she added, "Let's dig it up and see what it is."

"Hey!" Ellie shouted, with glee, as she got up to hunt for a thick stick too, "I was thinking that same thought!"

When they both had their sticks, they went back to… whatever it was and began digging. They dug and dug and du… okay, so you know what they did. When they had dug enough dirt away from its edges to loosen it from the ground, Ellie picked it up and exclaimed, "It is a rock! But what kind?"

Lucy took a closer look at it and replied, "Well, as I said, I have never actually seen a rock like this, but I have seen pictures of granite rocks, and that is what it looks like to me."

"Oh, wow," Ellie said, "I like the way it looks and the way it feels. It is rough, but not really scratchy."

"It is pretty," Lucy agreed.

Then, as Ellie brushed off the rest of the dirt, which was quite a bit, something fell to the ground. She stooped down, picked it up, brushed the dirt off of it, and excitedly said, "Oh my goodness, look at this!"

As Lucy stepped closer, Ellie held up a coin. "This is a Buffalo Nickle! My Daddy has some of these in his coin collection! Isn't it awesome?!"

Lucy looked at it with curiosity, but not with the same kind of enthusiasm as Ellie was expressing, and replied, "Yeah, it is pretty nice."

"I am going to keep it and the rock," Ellie said joyfully. But then, before putting it into her shoulder bag, she said to Lucy, "Unless you want them."

"No," Lucy replied, "You keep them. After all, you were the one who found them and it is obvious to me that they have more meaning to you than they do to me."

"Are you sure?" Ellie asked, not wanting to be greedy. "They are pretty cool treasures!"

"Yes, I am sure," Lucy responded, with a smile and a little bit of a chuckle.

As Ellie put both the rock and the coin into her shoulder bag, they turned back to the trail and continued up Y Mountain. However, it was not too long before Ellie exclaimed, with what sounded like a tad bit of alarm and a heap of curiosity, "Oh, my goodness! What is that?"

"What is what?" Lucy asked, not seeing what Ellie was looking at.

"That!" Ellie responded, pointing to what she saw but without taking even a tiny step closer to it. "It looks like a rubber hose, but it is moving."

Looking in the direction to which Ellie was pointing, Lucy could now see what Ellie saw; it was a snake!

"Oh," Lucy said, "I think that is a Rubber Boa Snake. I have seen those before when hiking with my dad, and that is what he called them."

"Well," Ellie said, in an unsettled tone, as she walked to the other side of the trail and continued up the mountain, "I do not like snakes! Nope!! Not at all!!! Never have!!!! Well, a least not since I was at Camp Fire Resident Camp, and a snake wrapped itself around my leg when I was in the lake for swim lessons! That was really scary! So, no! I do not like them! They are nothing but a threat to my sense of peacefulness!"

"Ellie," Lucy said with amusement. "You are a nut!"

"Yep!" Ellie agreed. "A pistachio nut!!"

"What?" Lucy asked.

"A pistachio nut!" Ellie explained. "They are Italian nuts, 100% Italian. And I am Italian, 100% Italian. So, if I am a nut, and since I am Italian, I must be a pistachio nut!"

"Oh my gosh!" Lucy laughed.

Now, of course, as they continued to the top of Y Mountain and then back down, they also continued their search, mostly off the trail, for whatever there was to see. And while they did see lots of different kinds of rocks, many beautiful plants, trees, shrubs, numerous different animals, and a lot of birds, they did not find any other treasures or threats. Nope! All they did find was nothing, just nothing!

Okay, now that you know what I meant by treasures, threats, and nothing, I will go back to where I was and continue what I was saying.

Ellie really did love hiking and, as I said before, the Y Mountain trail was her favorite trail to hike. Now, of course, she had not had the opportunity to hike too many other trails, only two, I think, or maybe three, and she loved them all. But the Y Mountain Trail was her most preferred. She loved its steepness, its openness, its panoramic view. She loved that it was close enough for her to get to it without a car, which she did not have, and she loved the Y. The great big white letter Y painted on the side of the mountain, very close to the top that served as an insignia for BYU.

When she got to the top, though the snow was not deep, there was enough of it on the ground for Ellie to make the wiser choice to just stand at the top of the big white letter Y rather than sit down on it like she usually did, and gaze at the awesome view of the BYU campus, of Provo, of Orem, of... well let me cut this short and just say it was the awesome view of everything that could be seen from the top of Y Mountain. And, as she enjoyed the view, she also thought, and thought, and tho... well, I think you know what I mean. She thought about many of the wonderful things that she had experienced since being baptized into The Church of Jesus Christ of Latter-Day Saints.

For one thing, she thought about the time, when she was just three months. Well not quite three, but close enough to call it that. After her baptism, when the Achsons, a family from church, took her with them to Palmyra, New York, to the Sacred Grove, where Joseph Smith had been visited by Heavenly Father and Jesus the Christ. Ellie remembered the wonderfully peaceful feeling she had had there. She could not remember anything in her life, at least up to that point, that had ever felt so good!

They also went to the place where the Golden Plates had been buried. Again, she recalled the wonderfully comforting feeling that had come over her there too. And, of course, she had been awed by the Hill Cumorah Pageant, a dramatization of some of the events recorded in the Book of Mormon, the visitation of Christ to the American Continent after He had been resurrected, and the restoration of the Gospel in these latter days. She had absolutely loved it all!!

But of all the memories that returned to her mind as she stood at the top of the big white letter Y, the memory that was most prominent and meaningful to her, the one she focused on the longest, was that of singing a song, word perfectly, that she had never even heard before!

'Uhhhh, how could she do that?' you are asking.

Well, here is your answer.

Harold B. Lee, who was the Prophet and the President of The Church of Jesus Christ of Latter-Day Saints then, had come to Palmyra and was there, at Hill Cumorah, to see the pageant that night. Chairs were set up for him and those who were with him. Once they were all seated and waiting for the pageant to begin, people began to gather around, outside the ropes, so they could wave to him and say hi.

Well, Ellie went over there too, but she did not wave or say anything. She just watched him, wishing that she could actually, in person, say hello to him. Then, at the exact moment that she had that thought, suddenly, he sat straight up on his chair, turned his head, and looked directly at her. Then he gave her a full, pleasing smile! And Ellie returned the same to him!!!!

She wondered if he actually knew what she had been thinking. And then, after just a brief moment, she realized that it was the Holy Spirit who told him where Ellie was and what she desired. And he had been happy to respond so he could make her happy.

It was at that time that someone in the crowd said, "Let's sing the Primary song, 'I Am a Child of God.' I understand that that is his favorite song. So, they all began singing. And so did Ellie!

Now, as I said before, she had not even heard that song yet, but as they sang, she sang too, every word of every verse, and she never forgot one word of that song after that! Oh! And yes, she also knew that it was the Holy Spirit that had taught her that song as she sang it.

Ellie walked a little farther up Y Mountain, to the actual top of the mountain, found a rock, a big rock that for some reason had no snow on it, and sat down. She looked up the sky, the clear blue sky that radiated with the sun's bright rays. As she did, she thought about some of the things she had been able to do as a student at the Y.

She thought about all her interactions as a dancer on the International Ballroom Dance Team and the Folk Dance Team. She recalled having been a part of many Square Dance performances. And she reminisced about her Latin Ballroom Dance experiences too. She expressed her gratitude to Heavenly Father for those opportunities because not only did she truly enjoy those experiences, but they provided opportunities she had never thought she would have.

You see, Ellie was quite picky about the type of dancing that she would do. So, until then, her BYU experiences, she had not had the opportunity to do any dancing beyond what she and her friends had done at their high school dances.

Now, those were not the only things that Ellie reminisced over. She also thought about some of her most favorite classes, like Family Relationships, Child Development, Fitness, Personal Health, Italian, and others, and all the appreciation she had for all that she had learned. But, of all the courses she had taken, she appreciated most, her religion classes! She had learned so much about the Bible, Old and New Testaments, the Book of Mormon, the Doctrine and Covenants, the Peal of Great Price, and so much more. And that she knew without a doubt, would help her throughout the whole of her life more than anything else she had learned or experienced.

Now, as Ellie thought about all the classes, activities, and adventures that had been a part of her BYU experience, she began to sigh. So deeply had she been pondering that she came to the realization that, while she had done pretty good, Ellie knew that she had not done as well as she could have. So, after a few more moments, she got up and started walking down Y Mountain Trail, talking to Heavenly Father as she walked.

"Heavenly Father, I know that in some things I did very well. But I also know that in other things, I did not do well at all. At least not as well as I could have."

About halfway down the trail, Ellie paused. She looked up at the sky, sighed, and then said, "Heavenly Father, I could have done better, if I had done things right! I think the reason I did not do better than I did in some of the things that I took on, at least one of the reasons, was because I tried to do too much, more than was possible or realistic, to be done all at the same time. I guess I did not realize it then, but I sure do see it now. I put so much on my schedule each semester and term that I did not have enough time, all of the time I needed, to put into each class. So, while I did do really well in some of them, I know I did not do well enough in others."

Then, after another thoughtful pause, she added, "Hmmm, I guess another good lesson came out of that too, because now I see the great importance of being realistic. It is better to do less and do it well, the best that you can do, than to do more and do it poorly. Not as well as you could do. Hmmm, yes! I think that is one of the best lessons of all the lessons I have learned, because that will help me to always do better in all that I do, every time I do anything at all."

Again, looking up at the heavens, she said, with a loving expression of gratitude, "Thank you, Heavenly Father, for helping me to see what I have gained. Because *now I know* that I did not fail! Now, my grades were not that bad, but they were not as good as they should have been and could have been if I had done things differently. Still, right now, I feel the lesson I have just realized makes the struggle that brought it about worth it! And I am certain that as I progress through life and look back on these experiences and others that I have had and will have, I will continue to learn and learn and le . . . well, of course Thou does know what I mean! After all, Thou is the one who pointed it out to me!"

As Ellie made her way down the trail, she continued to think about many other things she had done, learned, enjoyed, and obtained as a student at BYU. She considered the many struggles she had faced and the various awards she had received. Ellie thought about the people she had come to love and appreciate: fellow students, teachers, members of her church wards and branches, and others. She pondered the great expanse of emotions that she had felt in various different types of circumstances. And in all of that, she could see that there had been something good to take away from every experience she had had, whether it was good or not so good, or even not as good as that!

Once off the trail, as she walked, not back to her apartment but to the Provo Temple grounds. She expressed her truly sincere gratitude to Heavenly Father. "I could never thank Thee enough for blessing me with Thy gospel," she began. "It has made such a magnificent difference in my life. And, one of the greatest blessings that it will, as long as I do my part, provide for me is that of Eternal Life with Thee, Heavenly Mother, Jehovah, my families, and everyone else who gains and lives Thy gospel! Thank you, Father! Thank you!! Thank you!!! Thank you!!!!"

All the way up to the temple grounds, Ellie sang. She sang songs she had learned for the choir performances she had been in. She sang hymns she had learned for Sacrament Meetings. She sang songs from her childhood and songs from her teen years. She sang because she was feeling so very happy! It had been, as it always was, a great comfort to talk with Heavenly Father. So yes, she was feeling quite good!

'Wait a minute!' You are screaming again. 'You told us that Ellie had a bit of sadness and a bundle of joy, but you never told us why. You also told us that she might not have the opportunity to hike the Y Mountain Trail again, but you never told us why. Do you not think you should clarify that?'

Oh, figeldy-wigeldy, I forgot about that. I guess I should, so I will.

Ellie was getting ready to leave BYU. In fact, she was getting ready to leave Provo. In double fact, Ellie was getting ready to leave Utah. And that made her quite sad because she really did want to finish school.

But she had just gotten engaged to a guy she did not really even know. So, because he is in the Air Force and is stationed at the Lowry Air Force Base in Denver, Colorado, she is going to move to Colorado. That way, they can spend some time together and get to know each other better before they actually do get married. And getting married is something Ellie really wants to do more than anything else! So, that is what filled her with joy!

Now, I shall move on!

Once on the temple grounds, Ellie walked the path from the back of the Provo Temple to the front of the Provo Temple and, seeing that the snow had been cleared off of all the benches and that they were dry, she sat down on the one that faced the front temple wall. As she looked up at the wall, focusing on the words House of the Lord, Holiness to the Lord, The Church of Jesus Christ of Latter-Day Saints, Ellie recalled that beautiful experience she had one day in January 1974, the day she gained her testimony of the gospel and of the church.

Hmmm... maybe I should share that story with you. Would you like me to do that? You would? Okay, I will!

When Ellie was baptized, she did not really know if the church and the gospel it taught were God's one true church and gospel; she hoped they were; she believed they were, but she could not really say she knew that they were. After being at BYU for only about three weeks, and because her homesickness was so intense, she decided that she had to know because if it was not true, she wanted to go home. So, she went up to the temple grounds to pray.

At the front of the temple, she knelt-down on the cold, hard, stone-paved path, and began praying. She prayed, and prayed, and prayed, and... well, you get the idea. Yet, there was nothing, no answer, no whisper, no feeling of any type.

Because she had been there for quite some time, and she was beyond freezing, she decided to go back to her dorm, warm up, and then return to the temple and continue to pray. But just as she was about to leave, there appeared a glow on the front temple wall. The words, House of the Lord, Holiness to the Lord, The Church of Jesus Christ of Latter-Day Saints, shimmered and shined in a way that nothing could. She blinked a few times, thinking that her eyes were playing tricks on her, and then looked again. That time, as she gazed intently, the words, The Church of

Jesus Christ of Latter-Day Saints, seemed to lift off
the wall and, appearing as little torches, float towards
her.

HOUSE OF THE LORD
HOLINESS TO THE LORD
THE CHURCH OF JESUS CHRIST
OF LATTER-DAY SAINTS

So real did they appear that, when they were just in front of her, above her head, she reached up to touch them. As she did, one by one, they fell, and as each one fell, a feeling of warmth, that burning feeling of the spirit, grew inside of her. When the last torch fell, with a full heart, tears of joy, an overarching peace, and a crystal clarity of mind, she knew that The Church of Jesus Christ of Latter-Day Saints is indeed the one true church of our one and only God, and that the gospel it teaches is the infinite, undeniable, living word of that God!

From that time on, she never, no never, questioned, doubted, or wondered if she had the truth. She knew that she did and she lived up to it. Because of that, she knew that if all her family did the same thing, they could and would be **together forever!** And nothing could make her happier than that! Ellie loved her family and she wanted them to always be together as a family, forever!

Okay, so now that you know all of that, it should make a world of sense to you to know that the Provo Temple held a very special place in Ellie's heart! Also, she loved being a student at BYU. And as you already know, she very much enjoyed walking the trails and hiking in the mountains! So, that should add you your understanding of what made her a little bit sad.

But, at the same time, knowing that she would soon be married for time and all eternity and could have her own family, all the children she had always wanted, and knowing how important that was to her, should also make it very clear to you why she was feeling happy!!

Now, it was getting a little late and Ellie had a lot of things to get done. So she got up from the bench, left the temple grounds, and headed back to her apartment. As Ellie walked, she thought about all the wonderful feelings that she had experienced both on Y Mountain and on the temple grounds. Again, looking up at the sky, with joy in heart and a grand smile on her face, she said, "I am so happy to have Thy gospel to guide me through this life, and I am inexpressibly grateful for the blessings that it provides. Especially the opportunity we, with our families and everyone else who follows Thy plan. To once again, after this life, return to be with Thee, Heavenly Father, and with Heavenly Mother, and with Jehovah. Nothing could bring more joy! After all, *That Is Where Home Is*, and home is where I want to be, with all of my family **together forever!**

# About the Author

Eileen DiStasio-Clark is the second oldest of four children. She is the mother of eleven children and grandmother to twenty-three grandchildren, to date. As a member of The Church of Jesus Christ of Latter-Day Saints, she serves in various positions, teaching, leading, and ministering to children, youth, and adults. Currently, she is also a Family History Missionary. Eileen established the Pursuit of Excellence Institute of Family Education, a non-profit organization focused on strengthening the family. Presently she holds an A.A., a B.A., and an M.A. in Clinical Psychology and is working on the completion of her Doctoral Degree.